タイ国民話

ピクンの花
「金の言葉を話すお姫さま」

Pikun Flowers　　The Princess of Golden Words
齋藤佐知子（作・画・翻訳）　　by Sachiko Saito

長崎文献社　　Nagasakibunkensha

1

　むかしむかし、ピクントーンという名前の娘がいました。ピクントーンというのは、タイ国の言葉で、金のピクンの花という意味です。どうしてそういう名前がついたかというと、こんなお話しがあったからなのです。

1

There was once a girl named Pikun-tong. Pikun-tong is a Thai name. It means gold flowers of pikun. How did she come to have this name? Find out by reading the story below.

ピクントーンは、おかあさんとおねえさんのマリと暮らしていました。
おとうさんは、ずっと前に亡くなってしまいました。
ピクントーンのおかあさんは、顔も姿も醜くて、自分のことしか考えていないような人でした。
そのうえ、言葉使いも乱暴で、すぐに口ぎたなくののしるのです。
おねえさんのマリは、おかあさんにそっくりで、おかあさんを小さくしたようでした。
ピクントーンはおとうさんに似て、器量よしだし、気立てもよいし、物腰もことばづかいも美しい娘でした。

2

Pikun-tong lived with her mother and her sister Mali. Her dear father passed away when she was a child.

Her mother was ugly and ill-natured. She only thought about her own desires, talked loudly, and abused her. Mali looked like her mother in both looks and personality. Pikun-tong looked like her father. She was beautiful and good-natured, kind with pleasant manner. She always spoke softly.

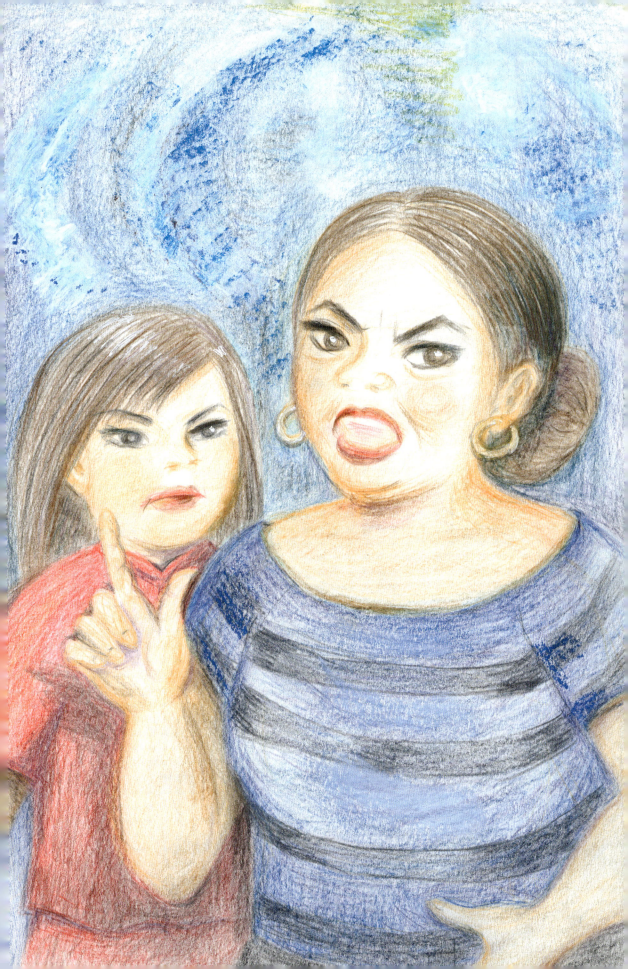

おかあさんは、自分にそっくりなおねえさんがかわいくてたまりませんでしたが、ピクントーンのことは大きらいでした。
おねえさんには仕事などさせずに遊ばせておきました。
仕事をさせるときには、簡単な仕事だけでした。
ところが、ピクントーンには、水くみ、米つき、……。

3

　So, her mother adored her sister who was the same image of her, but she disliked Pikun-tong. Mali was allowed to please herself most of the time and was only given easy tasks when asked to work by her mother.
　On the other hand, her mother made Pikun-tong work hard at fetching water from the river, polishing rice,

畑仕事など、たいへんな仕事ばかりをさせました。

4

and she was also made to work all day long in the fields.

ある晩のことです。ピクントーンは川へ水くみに行きました。川は家からずーっと遠く離れた山のふもとを流れています。
川から水をくみ、いっぱいになった水がめを肩にかついで、ピクントーンは一歩一歩足をふみしめながら歩いてきました。
暗い夜道はこわいから早く行きたいのに、水がめが重くて、思うように足が動いてくれないのです。

5

　One evening, Pikun-tong was sent to get water from the river which ran at the foot of a mountain quite a way from her home.
　On her return, she had to carry a heavy jar full of water on her shoulder and take care not to spill a drop.
　She became increasingly fearful of darkness at night, so she tried to walk faster but the weight of the water jar on her shoulder made this very difficult.

やがて、大きな木のところまでくると、おばあさんがすわっていて声をかけてきました。
「娘さん、水をくださらんかの」
ピクントーンはにっこり笑い、「おばあさん、どうぞいくらでもめしあがってください」といって、重い水がめをおろしてあげました。
おばあさんは、おいしそうに、水を飲み、ほっと息をついて、いいました。
「どうもありがとう。あなたは、親切な娘さんだ。それに言葉も美しい。ばばのそばにおいで。ごほうびをあげよう」
このおばあさんは、ほんとうは、この大きな木の精霊だったのです。
「心やさしく、言葉のきれいなあなたには、ひとことしゃべるたびに、口から金のピクンの花がこぼれおちるようにしてあげよう」
こういうと、おばあさんは消えてしまいました。悲しいことの多かったピクントーンは、うれしくて、「ありがとうございます」といいながら、その木に向かって、長いことひれ伏していました。

6

After a while she passed a big tree where an old woman sat. The old woman asked,

"Would you please spare some of your water for me?"

Pikun-tong smiled, saying,

"Please drink as much as you like."

She lowered the heavy jar from her shoulder.

The old woman happily drank water, sighed with relief and said to Pikun-tong,

"Thank you so much. You are so kind, and you speak so softly and beautifully. Come closer to me. I would like to reward you."

In fact, this old woman was a tree spirit living in the tree.

"Kind-hearted girl with golden words. From this moment whenever you speak, a gold pikun flower will fall from your mouth."

Then, the old woman vanished. Her deep sadness was immediately changed into happiness. In gratitude, she threw herself at the foot of the tree saying, "Thank you so much for your reward."

7

家へ帰ってくると、おかあさんの声がとんできました。
「こんな水くみぐらいになん時間かかっているんだい。ぐず！」
ピクントーンは、「申しわけありません」と小さな声であやまりました。すると、口から、金のピクンの花が、はらりと落ちてきたのです。おかあさんは驚き、目がぎょろぎょろぎらぎらしはじめ、醜い顔がますます醜くなりました。
「これはなんだ。あれっ。ピクンの花じゃないか。しかも金だよ。おまえの口から出てきたのかい。ほんとうに。いったいどこに行って来たんだい。かわいいあたしの娘や」

7

As soon as she entered the house she heard her mother shout,

"How long does it take you to get water? Ha? You lazy, good-for-nothing, slowcoach!"

Pikun-tong said, "I'm sorry, Mother," and a gold pikun flower fell from her lips. How surprised her mother was! She goggled so much that her distorted face seemed even uglier.

"What is this? Oh! It is a pikun flower…. made from gold! Did it come from your mouth? Really, truly? Well, well! Tell me my dearest daughter. Where have you been?"

ピクントーンがその晩あったことを話すと、そのたびに金のピクンの花が口からこぼれ落ち、おかあさんは、床をはいずりまわってかき集めました。話し終えると、おかあさんはせかせかと嬉しそうに、優しい声でいいました。
「あたしは、金持ちになる日が楽しみだ。かわいい娘や。もうおまえには、何もさせない。座って、かあさんと話をしていりゃいいんだよ」
おかあさんは、ピクントーンに昼も夜も話をさせました。しまう場所もないほど金は集まりましたが、おかあさんはもっとたくさん欲しくて、しゃべらせ続けるので、ピクントーンは疲れはててしまいました。少しでも休もうものなら、しかられたり、たたかれたりするので、かわいそうに、声がつぶれて、金のピクンの花も出なくなってしまいました。

8

Pikun-tong told her mother everything that had happened to her that evening. With each word a gold pikun flower dropped from her lips. Her mother crept along the floor hungrily gathering the flowers as they fell. When Pikun-tong had finished her story, her mother was happy and restless, and said in a gentle voice,

"I can count on the day when you will make me rich, my dearest daughter. You no longer have to work so hard for me. All you need to do is to sit and speak to your mother."

Her mother made her speak all day and all night. She got so many gold flowers that she soon ran out of space to store them all. Yet she wanted more, so Pikun-tong was made to continue speaking until she was exhausted. Her mother would scold and beat her when she tried to take a rest, so she completely lost her voice, and the gold flowers stopped coming out of her mouth.

さあ困った。おかあさんは、すわりこみ、考に考えて、いいことを思いつきました。
「そうだ、マリを水くみにいかせりゃいいのさ。きっと、年寄りの精霊に会って、ほうびがもらえるだろう」
おかあさんは、大声でマリを呼びました。マリがのそのそやってきました。
「マリや、ピクントーンが、どうやって金のピクンの花を手に入れたか知ってるかい。おまえも少しは欲しいと思わないかい」
マリは、なまけ者の、ぼんやり屋でした。
「あたい、そんなことぜんぜん知らないよ。おかあちゃんは知ってるのかい」
おかあさんは、ピクントーンから聞いたことを話して聞かせました。
「なーんだ。そんなかんたんなことか。じゃ、あたい、今すぐ行ってくるわ」
おかあさんは、もう、わくわくしていいました。
「行きな。今すぐ。いそいで、いそいで」
マリは、銀製の上等な水がめを持って行きました。

9

　　Now. Her mother was very upset. She sat on the floor, and thought and thought what to do now. Then she hit upon a clever idea.
　　"I shall send Mali down to the river for water, then she too will see the old spirit woman and be offered a reward."
　　Her mother called Mali in her loudest voice. Mali came in an unwieldy manner.
　　"Mali, do you know how Pikun-tong found the gold pikun flowers? Wouldn't you like some, too?"
　　Mali was lazy and dim witted. She replied,
　　"I don't know about that at all. Do you know, Mom?" Her mother then explained everything Pikun-tong had told her.
　　"Oh, it's easy-peasy. I'll go to the river to get water now."
　　Her mother's heart beat faster and she said, "Go for it now, Mali. Quickly, quickly. Mali was given a valuable silver jar, and went to the river.

水をくみ終えて、いよいよ大きな木のところへやって来ると、虹のようにきれいな着物をまとった、輝くばかりに美しい女の人が立っていて、水を欲しいとたのむではありませんか。
おかあさんがいったような、おばあさんではなかったし、それに、自分よりきれいな女の人は大きらいだったので、マリは、つんつんしていいました。
「おまえのために水をくんできたんじゃあないんだよ。あたいの銀の水がめの水を飲もうったって、そうはいかないよ。飲みたいなら、自分で飲んできなよ」
ほんとうは、その女の人は、ピクントーンにほうびをくれた精霊だったのです。マリが逃げてゆこうとすると、女の人が呼びとめました。
「ちょっとお待ちなさい。まあ、あなたは、ずいぶん乱暴な人ね。でも、わたしは、あなたにも、ごほうびをあげましょう。けれど、悪いことば使いへのごほうびです。今からは、一こと話すたびに、ミミズやムカデが、口からこぼれ落ちるのです」
こういって、女の人は消えてしまいました。
マリは驚きました。ああ大変なことになった。

10

When she filled it with water, she walked and reached the big tree.

However, there was a shining woman in a beautiful dress the colors of the rainbow standing by it. The woman stopped her and asked for a drink. She was not the old woman as her mother had told her, and she was jealous of beautiful women, so she snapped unfriendly.

"I didn't make so much effort to get this water to share with the likes of you. No, I'll never give a drop to you from my silver jar. If you are thirsty, get your own drink!"

In fact, the woman was the same tree spirit that had offered the reward to Pikun-tong. When Mali was leaving, the woman reproached,

"Wait. How unkind of you! But I will still give you too a reward for your nasty, spiteful words. Listen. From now on, each time you speak, earthworms and centipedes will fall from your mouth."

When the woman had told her so, she vanished.

Mali stood in a state of shock. What a terrible thing happened!

11

おかあさんは、マリの帰りを今か今かと待っていました。遠くのほうにマリの姿が見えると、おかあさんは、待ち切れずに、
「どうだった、どんなほうびをもらってきたのかい」
と叫びながら、かけよりました。
マリは、途方にくれて、「ああ、おかあちゃん……」といいました。
すると、ミミズとムカデが、口からこぼれ落ちました。
マリが家に入って、起こったことを話すと、ひとこと話すたびに、ミミズやムカデが出てきて、とうとう家いっぱいになってしまいました。

11

  Her mother was waiting for her in expectation. When she saw Mali in the distance, she was running toward her shouting, "How was it, Mali? Did you get the reward?"
  Mali was at a loss for words and said,
  "Oh, Mom, oh Mom!"
  Then worms and centipedes fell from her mouth.
  Mali began to explain what had happened to her mother, so more and more worms and centipedes dropped from her mouth until there would be enough to fill the whole house.

これを見たおかあさんは、ピクントーンが話したこととちがうので、ピクントーンがにくらしくて、棒でなんどもたたきました。
ピクントーンは、こらえきれずに、逃げて、森にかくれました。

12

　　When her mother saw it, she became enraged and called Pikun-tong a liar and with a hatred of her she set about beating her with a stick until Pikun-tong was forced to flee into the forest.

ちょうどそのとき、この国の王子が、馬に乗って森へやってきました。
王子は、その前の晩、山のふもとを流れる川の近くへ馬に乗って散歩に来ていました。
そして、あの大きな木のところまでやってくると、おばあさんがすわっていて、王子を呼びとめてこんなことをいったのです。
「あすの朝、森へ散歩に行きなされ。あなたの妻になる人に出会うでしょう。その人は、話すたびに、口から金のピクンの花をこぼしますよ」
王子は、おばあさんのことばを信じて、朝になると、森へやってきたのでした。
そして、ピクントーンが木の下で泣いているところを通りかかりました。
王子は、馬をとめてたずねました。
「どうして、こんなところで泣いているのかね」
「私は、家から追い出されてしまったのでございます」

13

Just then the prince of this country came to the forest exercising his horse.

The previous night the prince was riding on the horse near the river at the foot of the mountain.

He had met the old woman when he reached the big tree. He had been stopped by the old woman sitting beside the big tree. She had said to him,

"If you return to this place tomorrow morning, you will meet a girl who is your bride-to-be. You will know her by the gold flowers that fall from her mouth each time she speaks.

The prince trusted her and came to the forest on horse in the morning. He saw Pikun-tong weeping under the tree. The prince stopped and asked,

"Why are you here weeping?"

"I had to leave my house," she explained.

ピクントーンが話すたびに、口から金のピクンの花がこぼれ落ちました。これを見た王子は、胸をはずませて、馬をおりて見にきました。手にとってみて、驚きました。
「金のピクンの花だ。本物の金のピクンの花だ。いったいどうしたのか話してごらん」
ピクントーンは、今までのことをすべて話しました。それを聞き終えると、王子は喜んで叫びました。
「そうか、あなたなのだね。私の妻になる人は。さあ、わたしといっしょに行こう」
王子は、夕べあったことをピクントーンに話して聞かせました。
そして、ピクントーンを、あの大きな木の前につれて行き、二人を会わせてくれたことを感謝して、その木に向かって深くひれ伏したのでした。

14

    With each word, a gold pikun flower fell from her mouth. The prince was astonished! He came closer, picking up one of the gold pikun flowers he said,
    "This is a gold pikun flower, a real one! Please tell me what happened to you."
    Pikun-tong told him everything. After he heard her story, he exclaimed,
    "That's you! You are my bride! Please come with me."
    The prince told her what had happened the previous night.
    He went to the big tree with Pikun-tong, and they bowed low to show their gratitude for meeting each other.

こうして、ピクントーンは、王子と結婚して、お城でしあわせに暮らしたということです。

（おわり）

15

　Shortly afterwards, Pikun-tong married her prince and they lived together happy in his big castle.

(The End)

著者あとがき

　「ピクントーン」はタイ国のナコンサワン県で採取された民話です。民話の話型としては、AT（アールネ・トンプソンの型番号）403「黒い花嫁と白い花嫁」と同じカテゴリーに入ります。この型の民話には継子いじめが多いのですが、「ピクントーン」では、母親が実の娘を虐待します。

　シンデレラ物語をはじめ、これに似た話型の民話は世界中にありますが、「ピクントーン」のタイらしい特徴は、ピイーという精霊が出てくることでしょう。タイにはピイー信仰という精霊崇拝があり、自然界のさまざまな事物にピイーが宿っていて、人間に恩恵を与えたり、逆に、災いをもたらしたりすると信じられています。タイの人々はピイーに対して畏敬の念や恐怖感を持っています。この話の中で、大きな木の精霊が心根のよいピクントーンには幸運をもたらしてくれましたが、ピイーの心に沿わなかったマリには災いをもたらしました。

　私が民話に魅せられたのは、幼少のころにさかのぼります。寝る前に母が私たち子どもに読み聞かせたお話しの本の中に数々の民話がありました。それは毎晩楽しみにしていた時間でした。それから長い年月を経て、大学の卒業論文を書く時、民話がよみがえってきました。タイの民話を翻訳し、日本の民話と比較研究し、更に大学院で、タイ、ビルマ（ミャンマー）、ベトナムの民話を翻訳、比較しました。「ピクンの花」は、その時に翻訳した民話の一つです。

　民話はその名のとおり、民の話です。歴史教科書に登場することのない、庶民の生活、生きざま、思いなど、私たちの先祖の生活を垣間見ることのできるという点で興味深いものです。世界の遠く離れたところに同じような話が存在することも、人類の共通点を示すものとして感動的です。

　この話を通して、良くも悪くも言葉のもたらす結果の重大さを教えられます。大人にも子どもにも読んでほしいと思い絵本にしました。また、日本人だけではなく世界の人々にも知らせたいと思い英訳しました。

　この絵本を手に取られたみなさまが、この民話を楽しみながら何かを学んでいただければ幸いです。

Afterword

"Pikun-tong" is a folktale from Nakhon Sawan Province in Thailand. It belongs to AT (the Aarne-Thompson Type Index of Folk Tales) 403, in the same category as "The Black and White Brides". There are many stories about ill-treated stepchildren in this group, but in "Pikun-tong", the mother abuses her real daughter.

While various other stories, such as "Cinderella", belong to this category, "Pikun-tong" introduces a uniquely Thai characteristic when the spirit, or phi appears. Thai people believe that everything in nature houses phi, and phi bring either benefits or misfortunes to people. Therefore, phi are regarded with feelings of awe and respect or fear. In this story, while the spirit gave happiness to a kind girl, Pikun-tong, misfortune came to Mali, who made the spirit angry.

I was first attracted to folktales in my early days. My mother used to read children's stories to us before we went to sleep. It was the time I looked forward to. Later, while preparing my university graduation thesis, I made folktales the focus of my study. I translated Thai folktales and compared them with Japanese folktales. In graduate school, I translated Thai, Burmese and Vietnamese folktales and made a comparison. "Pikun-tong" is one of the folktales I translated at that time.

Folktales are stories by and about people. Reading them is interesting because we can get a glimpse of the lives of our ancestors, including ordinary people who never appear in history books – gaining insights into their lifestyles, attitudes toward life and other ideas. It is also moving because similar folktales exist in many faraway places of the world, suggesting that humankind is bound together by strong ties.

This story teaches us the important effects of the words we speak, both good and bad. I am presenting it as a picture book in Japanese and English so that it can be read by children as well as grown-ups, and by people in other counties as well as in Japan.

I hope you will enjoy the picture book and learn something important from it.

◆著者プロフィール
齋藤佐知子(さいとう　さちこ)
1943年、東京に生まれる。東京外国語大学、同大学院卒業。
大学卒業論文で、タイの民話を翻訳し、日本の民話と比較研究。
大学院でタイ、ビルマ(ミャンマー)、ベトナムの民話を翻訳、比較研究する。
卒業後、英語教師として現在に至る。
アジアの民話に限らず、後世に残したい心を打つ民話に絵を描いて絵本を執筆中。

◆発行日　2018年4月20日

ピクンの花　タイ国民話「金の言葉を話すお姫さま」

Pikun Flowers　The Princess of Golden Words

齋藤佐知子(作・画・翻訳)　　by Sachiko Saito

発行人	片山仁志
編集人	堀　憲昭
発行所	長崎文献社　Nagasakibunkensha

850-0057
長崎市大黒町3-1　長崎交通産業ビル5階
TEL 095-823-5247　Fax 095-823-5252
メール：nagasakibunkensha@gmail.com　info@e-bunken.com
ホームページ：http://wwwe-bunken.com

印　刷　シナノパブリッシングプレス㈱

ISBN978-4-88851-292-3 C0098
©2018、Sachiko Saito, Printed in Japan
◇無断転載、複写を禁じます。
◇定価は表紙に表示してあります。
◇落丁本、乱丁本は発行元にお送りください。送料当方負担でお取り換えします。